Usborne

Little First Stickers
Noah's Ark

Illustrated by Tilia Rand-Bell

Words by Caroline Young

Designed by Yasmin Faulkner

You'll find all the stickers at the back of the book.

Meet Noah and his family

Noah and his wife Emzara have three grown-up sons. Add some stickers to this page to see them all, with their wives.

Noah   Emzara

Noah and his family grow crops and keep animals.

Building the ark

One day, God told Noah that a big flood was coming. He told him to build a massive ship called an ark, and take his family, and two of all the animals on Earth inside it to stay safe.

There was a lot to do!

Woof!

Two by two

Noah led his family into the ark first. Then, he welcomed two of every kind of animal, one male and one female, just as God had told him to. It was an incredible sight.

Safely inside

It was very noisy in there, with all the roaring, chirping, croaking and hissing. At last, Noah closed the big door, and everyone began to settle down, just as the rain began.

The flood

It rained and rained and rained, without stopping, for 40 days and 40 nights. The whole land was covered with water.

On dry land

When the rain stopped, the ark was resting on some rocks. Everyone inside the ark was saved. Noah sent a dove out, and when it brought back a branch from a tree, he knew that the land was dry again.

The rainbow

As soon as he was sure that it was safe, Noah let all the animals out. When his family came out, they saw a beautiful rainbow in the sky. It was God's promise that there would never be another big flood.

New life

In time, all the animals from the ark had babies, and the Earth was bursting with new life. Noah had lots of grandchildren too, so he was very happy.

Meet Noah and his family pages 2–3

Japheth
Shem
Ham
chicks
cow
dog
ducks
sheep

Two by two pages 6–7

The flood pages 10–11

New life page 16

parrots

blackbirds

kingfishers

rabbits

horses

monkey

tortoise

crocodiles

dragonflies

lizard

deer

mouse

snails

butterflies